Recycle,
Reduce,
Reuse,
Rethink

Paper

Kate Walker

Smart Apple Media

This edition first published in 2005 in the United States of America by Smart Apple Media.

Smart Apple Media
1980 Lookout Drive
North Mankato
Minnesota 56003

Library of Congress Cataloging-in-Publication Data

Walker, Kate.
  Paper / by Kate Walker.
  p. cm. — (Recycle, reduce, reuse, rethink)
  Includes index.
  ISBN 1-58340-558-5 (alk. paper)
  1. Paper—Juvenile literature. 2. Papermaking—Juvenile literature. I. Title. II. Series.

  TS1105.5.W35 2004
  676'.042—dc22   2003070419

First Edition
9 8 7 6 5 4 3 2 1

First published in 2004 by
MACMILLAN EDUCATION AUSTRALIA PTY LTD
627 Chapel Street, South Yarra 3141

Associated companies and representatives throughout the world.

Edited by Helena Newton
Text and cover design by Cristina Neri, Canary Graphic Design
Technical illustrations and cartoons by Vaughan Duck
Photo research by Legend Images

Printed in China

Acknowledgements
The author and the publisher are grateful to the following for permission to reproduce copyright material:

Cover photograph: newspaper sorted for recycling, courtesy of Photodisc.

AAP/Associated Press AP/AP Photo/John McConnico, p. 14; Ted Mead/ANTphoto.com, p. 12; Artville, p. 5 (egg carton); Brand X Pictures, p. 5 (notebook); Corvallis-Benton County Public Library, p. 21; Der Grune Punkt – Duales System Deutschland AG, p. 20; Getty Images/Photodisc Blue, p. 18; Gibson Elementary, Canada, p. 25 (top); Great Southern Stock, p. 8; Annelise Koehler, www.alk-animals.com, p. 26; Dennis Sarson/Lochman Transparencies, p. 16; Photodisc, pp. 5 (box, newspaper stand), 11, 29 & design features; Dale Mann/Retrospect, pp. 9 (right), 25 (bottom); Reuters, p. 13; SCRAP (School Communities Recycling All Paper), p. 27; Terry Oakley/The Picture Source, pp. 19, 23; Tesco and the Woodland Trust, p. 24; The G.R. "Dick" Roberts Photo Library, p. 10; VISY Recycling, pp. 9 (left), 17, 22.

While every care has been taken to trace and acknowledge copyright, the publisher tenders their apologies for any accidental infringement where copyright has proved untraceable. Where the attempt has been unsuccessful, the publisher welcomes information that would redress the situation.

Contents

Let's start recycling now!

*When a word is printed in **bold**, you can look up its meaning in the glossary on page 31.*

Recycling

Recycling means using products and materials again to make new products instead of throwing them away.

Why recycle?

Developed countries have become known as "throw-away societies" because they use and throw away so many products, often after just one use! Single-use products include drink cans, glass jars, sheets of paper, and plastic bags. Today, there are approximately six billion people in the world. By the year 2050, there could be as many as nine billion people. The world's population is growing fast, and people are using a lot more products and materials than they did in the past.

Instead of throwing products away, we can recycle them. When we recycle:

- we use fewer of the Earth's **natural resources**
- manufacturing is "greener" because recycling creates less **pollution** than using **raw materials**
- we reduce waste, which is better for the environment.

Governments, industries, communities, and individuals all around the world are finding different ways to solve the problems of how to conserve resources, reduce manufacturing pollution and waste, and protect the environment. If the Earth is to support nine billion people in the future, it is important that we all start recycling now!

As well as recycling, we can:

- reduce the number of products and materials we use
- reuse products and materials
- rethink the way we use products and materials.

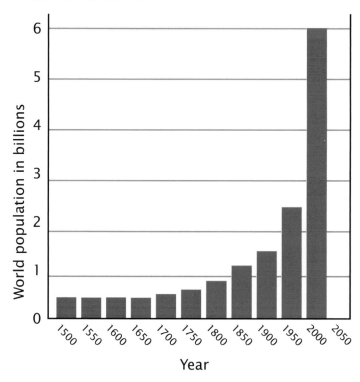

Today, there are more people on Earth using more products and materials than in the past, and the population is still growing.

What is paper?

Paper is the **pulp** of woody plants that has been finely shredded, mashed with water, and dried in flat sheets.

The history of paper

Paper was first made in A.D. 105 by a Chinese official named Ts'ai Lun. He mixed shredded rags with fibers from a plant called hemp and from mulberry bark, then pressed the pulp flat and dried it in the sunlight. The Chinese taught their neighbors, the Arabs, the art of paper making. As the Arabs moved westward across Europe, they took this knowledge with them. In 1719, a Frenchman, René-Antoine Ferchault de Réaumur, suggested that paper could be made from wood. He got the idea from watching some wasps, now called paper wasps, build their nest.

Large-scale production of cheap paper began in the mid-1800s, when chemicals were found that could soften the tough fibers of wood into pulp.

Paper products today

Today, most paper is made from wood pulp. Paper is used for:

- writing materials
- books and newspapers
- cardboard and paper packaging
- **insulation** material around power cables
- throw-away tissues, towels, and egg cartons
- throw-away clothes used in hospitals.

We use many of these paper products every day.

How paper is

Some paper is buried in **landfills** and some is recycled. The average household in a developed country throws away 514 pounds (233 kg) of paper each year.

The paper that is recycled goes through many processes.

People put their clean waste paper out for curbside collection.

The mixed waste paper is collected by a truck and taken to the recycling center.

At the recycling center, different types of paper are separated into pure streams of different grades.

NEWSPAPER

WHITE PAPER

CARDBOARD

The pure-stream papers are pressed into large bundles, called bales, and are sent to the paper mill.

recycled

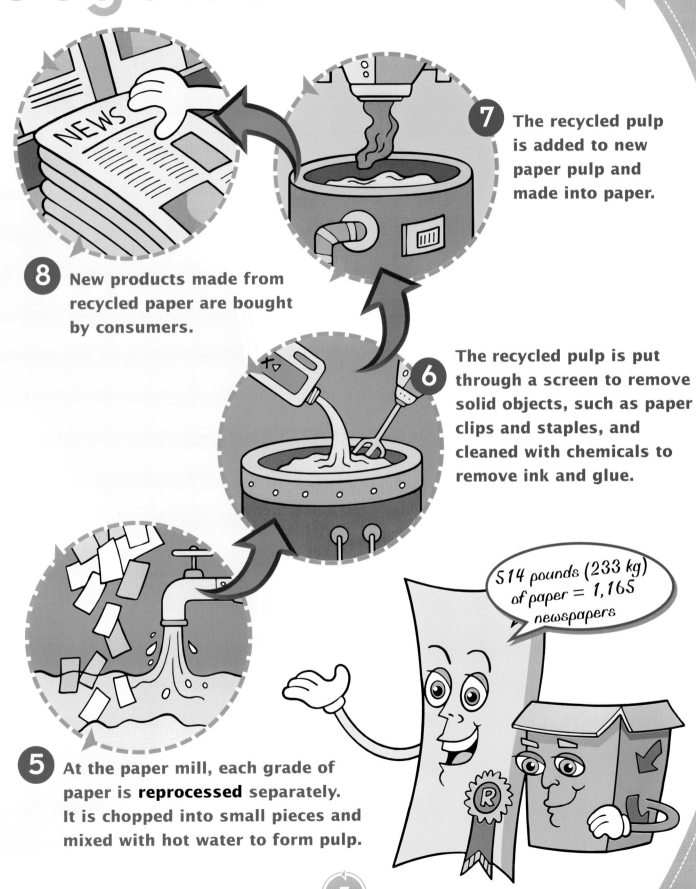

7 The recycled pulp is added to new paper pulp and made into paper.

8 New products made from recycled paper are bought by consumers.

The recycled pulp is put through a screen to remove solid objects, such as paper clips and staples, and cleaned with chemicals to remove ink and glue. **6**

514 pounds (233 kg) of paper = 1,165 newspapers

5 At the paper mill, each grade of paper is **reprocessed** separately. It is chopped into small pieces and mixed with hot water to form pulp.

Recycled paper

Used paper products can be recycled into the same products again, or made into very different products. There are two types of recycling: closed-loop and open-loop recycling.

Closed-loop recycling

Closed-loop recycling happens when used materials are remade into new products again and again. The materials go round in a non-stop loop and are never wasted.

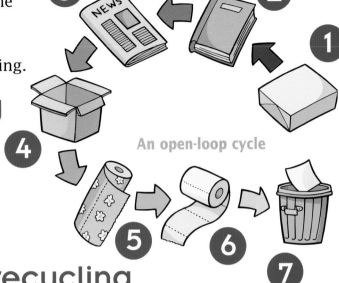

An open-loop cycle

Open-loop recycling

Open-loop recycling happens when used materials are made into different products that cannot be recycled again. The materials are usually only reused once, then thrown away.

Open-loop paper recycling

All paper is recycled in an open loop. Paper cannot be recycled in a continuous closed loop like steel, aluminum, or glass. Each time paper is reprocessed, its fibers become weaker and shorter. After being recycled several times, the weakened fibers get washed away in the de-inking process. All grades of paper can be reprocessed about seven times. After that, they are thrown away.

Glossy magazine paper is made by adding natural clay to pulped wood fibers. Glossy paper must be recycled separately and the clay removed. This is an expensive process.

Paper grades

Different grades of paper are usually recycled separately because they have different levels of whiteness and contain different fibers of different lengths and strengths. The five paper grades are:

- white paper, such as office paper
- colored paper used in magazines, junk mail, and **paperboard**
- brown paper, such as cardboard
- **newsprint** used for newspapers
- coated papers, such as glossy paper and waxed packaging.

products

High-grade recycled paper products

High-grade recycled paper is made by adding recycled paper pulp to new pulp. The strong fibers in the new pulp replace the weak fibers lost when the recycled pulp is de-inked. Each grade of paper is recycled separately. High-grade recycled paper products include:

- 🔄 **new office paper** This is made from used office paper.
- 🔄 **new cardboard boxes** These are made from used cardboard boxes.

Low-grade recycled paper products

Low-grade recycled paper products are made when no new paper pulp is added to a recycled batch. This means that high-quality paper products are recycled into low-quality paper products.

Low-grade products can also be made when papers of mixed grades are pulped together. Low-grade recycled products include:

- 🔄 **paper towels and tissues** These are made from used white paper.
- 🔄 **egg cartons** These are made from used papers of mixed grades.
- 🔄 **pellets for pet litter trays** These are made from used newsprint.

Other recycled paper products

Used paper is also made into a range of recycled products that look nothing like paper. These include:

- 🔄 **paper furniture** The pulp from mixed papers and cardboard is combined with strong glue and pressed into flat boards. These boards are cut like wood and made into furniture.
- 🔄 **plasterboard** The pulp from mixed papers is sandwiched either side of a layer of plaster to make plasterboard for walls and ceilings.

Furniture made from "paper" wood and plasterboard used for ceilings and walls are made from recycled paper, but cannot be recycled again.

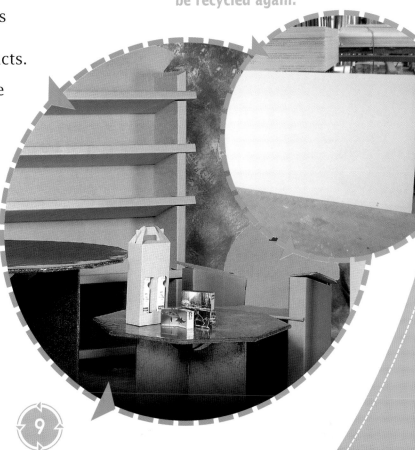

When used paper products are recycled to make new paper products:

- ♻ we use fewer of the Earth's natural resources
- ♻ manufacturing is "greener" because recycling creates less pollution than using raw materials
- ♻ we reduce waste, which is better for the environment.

Conserving natural resources

> When paper is recycled, trees are left to grow for people in the future to use.

Recycling is an important part of looking after the Earth's natural resources to make sure they are not wasted and do not run out. Natural resources are raw materials taken from the Earth and used to make products. Paper is made from the wood of trees. Trees are a **renewable** resource. When trees are cut down, new trees can be planted and grown to take their place. However, trees are being cut down faster than new ones can grow.

All around the world, whole forests of trees are being cut down to supply wood for paper making. Some of these forests have taken hundreds of years to grow. They are called old-growth forests. Big, heavy machines used to cut down forest trees also knock down other young trees in the area. This type of tree harvesting is called clearfelling and turns a forest into a bare slope. When paper is recycled, fewer trees are felled and less damage is done to the environment.

When forests are clearfelled to make paper, only a bare slope is left.

Paper is made from trees.

paper?

How felling trees affects the environment

Felling trees to make paper and other products affects the environment, because trees are needed for more than just making paper. Trees take in **carbon dioxide** gas and give out oxygen gas. Today, there is too much carbon dioxide in the atmosphere, partly because so many trees are being cut down. Carbon dioxide traps heat from the Sun and keeps the Earth's atmosphere warm. However, too much carbon dioxide has now trapped too much heat and caused **global warming**. Global warming has resulted in rising temperatures and has changed weather patterns worldwide, causing severe droughts, floods, and storms.

Trees also protect the land. Tree roots and decaying leaves help hold the soil in place and prevent it from being washed away by rain. When trees are felled and the soil is washed away, valuable plant food is lost. If the soil washes into rivers, it builds up and can stop the water from flowing freely. Trees and forests also provide **habitats** for different plants and animals, and are used to make homes for people.

When paper is recycled, trees are left to grow, helping to keep the planet healthy, and providing food and shelter for many living things.

Another reason to conserve forests is because they are places of great beauty.

"Greener" manufacturing

Recycling is a great way to reduce some of the problems caused when paper is manufactured. Paper that is not recycled is made in four steps:

1 Chipping: Tree logs are cut into small chips.

2 Pulping: Wood chips are pulped to break down the wood fibers and remove unwanted materials.

3 Bleaching: Naturally brown wood fibers are bleached to turn them white.

4 Paper making: Bleached fibers are made into rolls of paper.

Recycling paper is "greener" than manufacturing new paper products because fewer raw materials are used and fewer harmful chemicals are released into the environment.

How chipping and pulping affect the environment

Wood is cut into small chips by mechanical blades. The chips are "cooked" in hot water with strong chemicals. This breaks down the large fibers in the wood into smaller pieces and dissolves the lignin, which is the natural glue that holds the fibers together. The wood chips are turned into pulp.

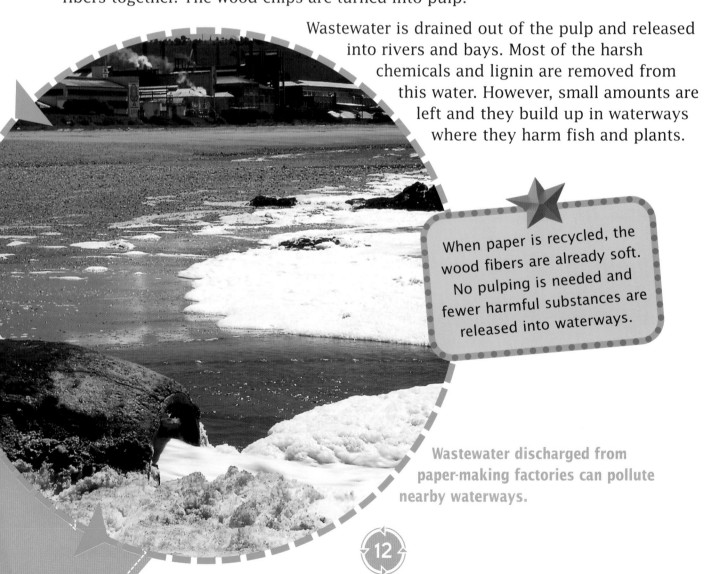

Wastewater is drained out of the pulp and released into rivers and bays. Most of the harsh chemicals and lignin are removed from this water. However, small amounts are left and they build up in waterways where they harm fish and plants.

When paper is recycled, the wood fibers are already soft. No pulping is needed and fewer harmful substances are released into waterways.

Wastewater discharged from paper-making factories can pollute nearby waterways.

How bleaching paper pulp affects the environment

Paper pulp is bleached to remove the brown color using **chlorine**, which is a very dangerous chemical. Chlorine mixes freely with other chemicals to form substances called dioxins. Dioxins are dangerous poisons that kill plants and cause cancer in humans. No matter how careful paper makers are, some chlorine always escapes into the environment. In paper-making accidents, chlorine gas can escape into the air, making people ill and harming plants and wildlife.

When paper is recycled, the fibers are already white, and only a small amount of chlorine bleach is used to reprocess them.

In 1996, a fire at a paper-making factory in Niderbipp, Switzerland, killed three firefighters. It took several days to put the fire out.

The ink is removed from recycled paper using mild detergent and not harsh chlorine.

Reducing waste

Billions of tons of paper are thrown away every year, creating troublesome waste. When paper is recycled instead of being thrown away, the amount of waste is reduced and some problems with waste are solved.

Paper in landfills

Landfills are large holes dug in the ground in which waste materials are buried. Paper and cardboard make up 25 percent of the volume, or amount of space, of all household waste sent to landfills. Paper is **organic** material that **decomposes**, or breaks down, naturally in air, releasing carbon dioxide gas. The solid part of paper returns to the soil as **compost**.

Paper buried in landfills is cut off from air, and decomposes differently. Instead of releasing carbon dioxide, it releases **methane**, a highly explosive gas. Methane often sets landfill sites on fire. Landfill fires can cause other kinds of waste, such as plastics, to burn. When plastics burn, dangerous gases are released into the atmosphere.

When paper is recycled, it is kept out of landfills. This reduces methane gas **emissions** and reduces the risk of landfill fires.

Methane and carbon dioxide gas trap heat from the Sun and add to global warming. Methane traps 25 times more heat than carbon dioxide.

The filters at this landfill site in Johannesburg, South Africa, clean methane gas created by decomposing paper and other organic material.

METHANE

CARBON DIOXIDE

The carbon cycle and paper waste

Paper was once living trees, and paper is made mainly of **carbon**. Carbon is one of the basic elements of the Earth, and all living things are made of carbon-based **molecules**. When living things die, they decompose and the carbon they contain returns to the soil as **humus**. Plants grow by taking up carbon from humus in the soil, and animals grow by eating plants or other animals, which all contain carbon.

It is important for the survival of all living things that large amounts of carbon move freely through this cycle, from one living thing to the next. When paper is sent to a landfill, it decomposes and becomes humus, however, it is buried too deep for plants to reach.

Paper sent to a landfill is buried deep underground where it is locked out of the carbon cycle.

When paper is recycled more trees are left to grow, so more carbon remains in the Earth's carbon cycle. Paper sent to a landfill is locked out of this cycle.

Plants take in carbon from humus in the soil.

Animals take in carbon by eating plants.

Dead plants and animals decompose and release carbon back into the soil as humus.

Paper in landfills decomposes into humus, but is buried too deep for plants to reach.

For and against

Question:

Can the Earth sustain its growing population?

Answer:

Yes, if people act now to preserve the environment and manage the Earth's resources better.

Question:

Can this be achieved just by recycling?

"YES" The "yes" case for recycling

✔ Recycling paper saves trees, which are vital to the health of the planet. Trees help reduce global warming. They protect soil and water, provide habitats for many different plants and animals, and are used to make homes for people.

✔ Recycling paper reduces the amount of harmful chemicals, such as chlorine, that escape into the environment and put plants, animals, and people at risk.

✔ Making paper from recycled material uses much less water and power than making paper from wood.

✔ Recycling paper keeps it out of landfills, where it takes up a lot of space and creates methane gas, which adds to global warming. Paper in landfills also creates risks of dangerous landfill fires and removes carbon from the Earth's carbon cycle.

People who are really committed to recycling paper take the time to sort and bundle different papers to make it easier for recyclers.

Papers of the same grade should be tied with string and never put in plastic bags.

recycling

Question:

Do most people agree that recycling is a good idea?

Answer:

Yes.

Question:

Will recycling fix all the problems caused by paper manufacturing and paper waste?

"NO" The "no" case against recycling

✗ Batches of paper for recycling can be **contaminated** by oil and food, plastic-coated papers, non-natural glues used to bind books and magazines, and sticky labels. Some of these contaminants produce poor-quality paper that has to be thrown away. Some contaminants can also clog paper-making machinery.

✗ Mixed papers collected from households are expensive to sort. Expensive sorting increases the cost of recycled paper products and this stops many people from buying them.

✗ Collecting heavy papers for recycling uses up valuable **fossil fuels**, which are **non-renewable** resources.

Many recycling plants still sort paper by hand. This is an expensive process.

✗ Recycled paper products often create a lot more waste because larger amounts of them are needed. Bathroom tissues and paper towels made from 100 percent recycled paper are not as strong and do not absorb as much water as products made from new materials.

✗ Some people think they can waste lots of paper just because paper can be recycled.

17

Reduce, reuse,

Recycling is a great idea, but it is just one answer to the problems of how to conserve resources, reduce manufacturing pollution and waste, and protect the environment. There are other things we can do that are even better than recycling. We can reduce, reuse, and rethink what we use.

Reduce

The best and quickest way to reduce paper waste is to use less paper! Reducing is easy. Some of the ways you can reduce paper use are to:

- buy fewer throw-away paper products, such as disposable tissues, towels, napkins, and plates
- stop using paper products that are not really needed, such as fancy notepads
- print out only documents that are really needed, and print single-spaced instead of double-spaced when using a computer
- write friends using e-mail instead of paper mail
- refuse to buy products with unnecessary paper or cardboard packaging
- write, telephone, or e-mail manufacturers and complain about unnecessary packaging. This may encourage them to use less.

You can save paper when you write friends using e-mail.

rethink

Reuse

A lot of paper products can be used again and again. Some of the ways paper products can be reused are:

- both sides of writing or typing paper can be used
- cardboard boxes can be used to store things or carry groceries
- books, magazines, and newspapers can be shared with family and friends
- unwanted books can be given to charity shops
- unwanted magazines can be given to doctors' and dentists' offices
- newspapers can be ripped up and spread on the garden as mulch, or added to the compost bin.

Shredded newspaper used as garden mulch holds moisture in the soil and saves water.

? Rethink

Everyone can come up with new ideas. Some ideas for changing the way we use paper products and materials are:

- governments can encourage people to recycle more paper by setting up more paper collection centers
- manufacturers can stop using harmful chemicals, such as chlorine, in paper making. Oxygen or ozone will bleach paper pulp just as well and cause less harm to the environment
- manufacturers can save trees by using non-wood materials for paper making, such as hemp plants
- schools and offices can stop using materials that contaminate paper for recycling, such as fluorescent papers and sticky labels
- shoppers can stop buying paper products that are non-recyclable, such as plastic-coated papers, foil-coated papers, and waxed papers.

What governments

Governments around the world are taking action to reduce paper waste and increase paper recycling. They are finding ways to recycle, reduce, and rethink paper use.

Recycle

Reduce

Rethink

Passing laws

In 1991, the government of the Republic of Germany passed a law called the *German Packaging Ordinance.* It was the first law of its kind in the world. It said that manufacturers had to take back all the packaging they put on their products. Germany decided to pass this law because:

↻ it wanted to discourage the large population of people from buying a lot of manufactured goods

↻ it wanted to prevent German manufacturers from putting a lot of fancy packaging on their products

↻ Germany had very little landfill space left in which to bury waste material.

The law was tough. It forced manufacturers to take back all packaging and reuse it or recycle it. Otherwise, they had to pay a large fee to have it **incinerated**. In just one year this law reduced the amount of packaging waste by an amazing 80 percent! Governments in other countries are thinking about passing similar laws.

DER GRÜNE PUNKT

GOVERNMENT APPROVED

The Green Dot symbol appears on German packaging to show that the manufacturer has paid for the packaging to be recycled or reused.

Recycle Reduce

Saving paper in a government-run library

The Corvallis Public Library in Oregon is two stories high. It covers an entire city block and is used by more than 2,000 people each day. Most libraries use a lot of paper, but not Corvallis. Workers have found simple ways to reduce paper use.

To make sure that all used paper is recycled, boxes for waste paper are placed next to all photocopiers, computer printers, and desks. Each floor of the building has one worker who makes sure that paper is sorted correctly and placed in the right recycling bins. The library has stopped using fluorescent-colored papers because they are not recyclable. Fluorescent papers also contaminate other recyclable papers.

In the past, the library posted out 50,000 notices to borrowers each year. A lot of paper was saved when notices were made 25 percent smaller. Now the library saves even more paper by sending notices by e-mail or leaving telephone messages. There are plans to replace folded paper handtowels in washrooms with paper handtowels on rolls. These rolls do not give out paper as easily or quickly as stacks of folded paper handtowels.

GOVERNMENT APPROVED

The Corvallis Public Library in Oregon has found ways to reduce its paper use and improve its paper recycling.

What industries are

Industries are getting better at reducing paper manufacturing waste and using fewer paper products. They are finding ways to recycle, reduce, reuse, and rethink their paper use.

Browser

Address http//:www.industry-updates.com   back forward home go

Favorites \ History \ Search \ Scrapbook \ Page Holder

Reuse Rethink

Turning waste into power

A new invention has changed what happens to paper sludge. Paper sludge is the waste material left over after recycled paper has been pulped and the ink removed. The sludge contains the paper fibers that have been recycled several times and are too weak and broken to be used again. For every 100 tons (91 t) of recycled paper that is de-inked, about 10 tons (9 t) of fiber is lost as sludge. In the past, most of this sludge was buried in landfills. There it took up valuable space and decomposed away from the air, creating dangerous methane gas.

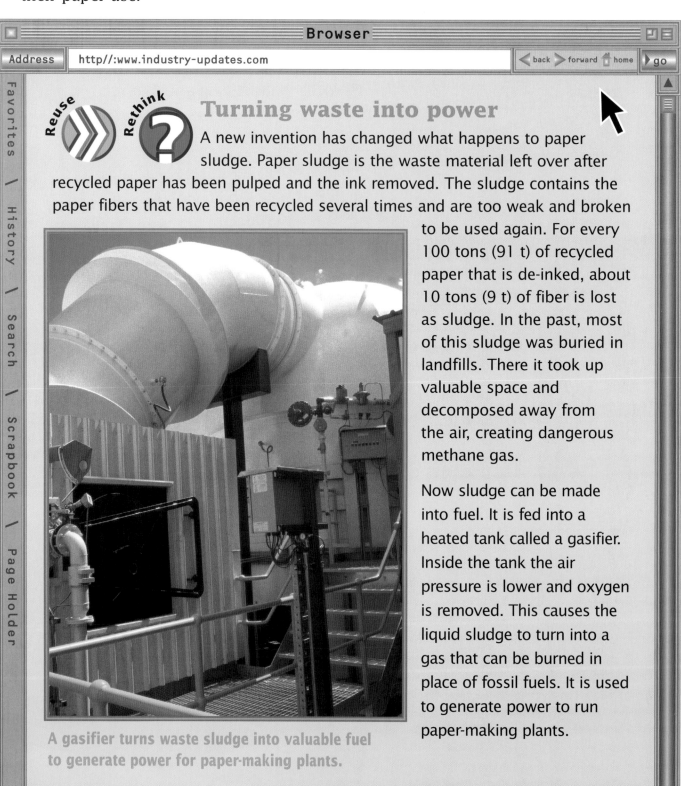

A gasifier turns waste sludge into valuable fuel to generate power for paper-making plants.

Now sludge can be made into fuel. It is fed into a heated tank called a gasifier. Inside the tank the air pressure is lower and oxygen is removed. This causes the liquid sludge to turn into a gas that can be burned in place of fossil fuels. It is used to generate power to run paper-making plants.

doing

Address | http//:www.industry-updates.com

Favorites \ History \ Search \ Scrapbook \ Page Holder

Rethink ❓

Making banana paper

In Central America, a company called Costa Rica Natural makes paper products from banana waste. Bananas are an important farm crop in Costa Rica. When bananas are cut from trees, about 253,350 tons (230,000 t) of woody stems are left over each year. Costa Rica Natural is taking the fiber from banana stems and adding it to recycled paper pulp. The banana fiber takes the place of new wood pulp, meaning new paper is produced without cutting down any more trees.

Paper products can be made using banana waste.

 Recycle **Reduce** **Reuse** **Rethink** ❓

Reducing paper use in shops

A chain of stores in New Zealand, called Farmers stores, are reducing their paper use in simple, clever ways:

- sales posters are reused at Christmas, Mother's Day, and Father's Day. The same basic poster is used each year with new features added
- office notepads are made from paper that has been used on one side
- stores in different parts of New Zealand run sales at different times, so that the same sale catalogs can be used by stores one after the other
- staff recycle all paper and cardboard boxes.

Some Farmers stores have reduced their waste paper by half!

What communities

Communities of people are working together to recycle and save a lot paper, and that saves a lot of trees!

Recycling Christmas cards

The Woodland Trust is a charity that creates and cares for native woodlands across the United Kingdom. Since 1999, the Woodland Trust has been involved in a program that recycles millions of used Christmas cards. They do this by working together with leading retail stores, a waste management business, and local government.

For four weeks after Christmas, people can bring used cards to WHSmith book and stationery stores, and Tesco supermarkets, and put them in special recycling bins. The cards are taken away and recycled into pulp. The Woodland Trust is not paid directly for recycling cards. Shop owners and landfill operators receive recycling tax credits from local governments for finding ways of keeping waste materials out of landfills.

The Woodland Trust 2002 Christmas Card Recycling Scheme collected 34 million cards. This kept 740 tons (671 t) of paper out of landfills and saved 11,407 trees.

These recycling tax credits fund the program. To date, this program has helped the Woodland Trust create and care for new woodlands at 28 sites across the United Kingdom.

ewspaper

Recycling aseptic packs

Square cardboard drink boxes, called aseptic packs, are made of 70 percent paper, 24 percent plastic, and six percent aluminum. Aseptic packs are good because they:

- use fewer raw materials than containers made of glass, plastic, or pure aluminum
- save energy because they are lightweight and pack closely together for transportation
- keep food fresh and do not have to be refrigerated until the container is opened.

In the past, only small quantites of aseptic packs were recycled because they make up a very small part of all household waste, just 0.03 percent.

Gibson Elementary students recycle many materials including aseptic packs.

Today, however, as countries around the world increase their recycling efforts, more aseptic packs are beng recycled to recover the paper and plastic.

In Canada, the governments of several provinces have put a deposit tax on aseptic packs to encourage people to save them for recycling. This prompted Grade Three students at Gibson Elementary School in Canada to save their aseptic packs, rinse them clean, and deliver them to the local recycling center. The students donate the deposit money to the World Wildlife Fund's "Adopt a Polar Bear" campaign.

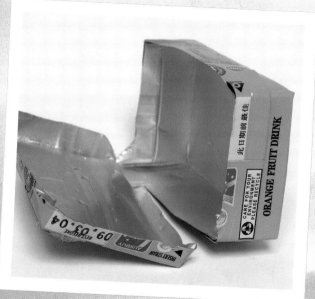

Aseptic packs are made of paper lined with aluminum-coated plastic.

What individuals are

Individuals are making a difference by recycling and reusing paper, whether they save whole forests or a single sheet of paper.

Individuals making your planet a better place.

Green Fingers Newsletter

Reuse

Making used paper sculptures

French artist, Anne-Lise Koehler, started sculpting because she wanted to capture the sense of wonder that filled her at the sight of wildlife, especially birds. Koehler begins a bird sculpture with two pieces of wire. She bends one piece into the shape of the beak, neck, back, and tail. She twists the other piece to make the legs. She uses a third piece of wire if the bird is to be shown with open wings. Koehler tears up used paper and fixes it to the wire with glue. Each layer of paper and glue must be left to dry before the next layer is added.

Koehler's sculptures are usually made of newspaper and typing paper. She has no way of telling how a sculpture will turn out, because different types of paper dry in different ways. Koehler paints some sculptures with acrylic paint and leaves others bare. Her aim is to capture the movement and expression of wild creatures.

Anne-Lise Koehler's sculptures are made of strips of used newsprint glued to a wire frame.

doing

SCRAP

Recycle

Recycling at school

In 1991, teachers at Holsworthy High School in Sydney, Australia, were worried about the large amount of waste paper going into school garbage bins and ending up in landfills. Three teachers did something about it. They contacted a recycler and found out how to get this paper recycled. They put boxes for paper collection in each classroom and staffroom. The paper was then stored in large wool bale holders. When six holders were filled, the recycler was called to collect them. Other schools heard about Holsworthy High's recycling efforts and started to do the same. Soon the project had a name, SCRAP.

In 2002, the Recycler of Year Award went to East Maitland Public School. Peter Carroll, one of the teachers who started SCRAP and runs it today, presented the award dressed as a frog.

Today, SCRAP has more than 1,500 schools and other organizations saving waste paper for recycling. In 12 years, SCRAP has recycled 55,115 tons (50,000 t) of paper, meaning they have saved more than 650,000 trees. SCRAP does more than recycle school waste. It also advises schools about "green" purchasing and how to avoid materials that harm the environment, and reduce and reuse all types of materials. SCRAP also holds annual environmental awards for schools, called the Froggies Awards.

What you can do

You can do all sorts of activities to help recycle, reduce, and reuse paper. You can also get others interested and come up with ideas to stop paper from harming the environment. Make a weekly "Paper 3-R scorecard" for yourself or your class.

What to do:

1 Draw up a scorecard with headings like the one shown below.

2 Write down each time you or your class do something to recycle, reduce, or reuse paper.

3 Reward yourself or your class with a green star for each activity that you do.

Paper 3-R scorecard

Recycle	Reduce	Reuse	Get others interested	Other things
Made a recycled paper box to keep under my desk.	Used a cloth handkerchief instead of paper tissues.	Used both sides of the paper for my local history interviews.	Talked to Grandma about recycling her newspapers instead of trashing them.	Put a sign on our letter box: "No junk mail please."
Recycled all my swimming club newsletters from last year.	I'm writing smaller.	Made notepads out of Mom's old reports.	Talked to my teacher about having a recycled paper bin in our class.	Got Dad to buy recycled paper toilet rolls.
	Kim and I agreed to buy one swimming magazine and share it.	Cut up last year's Christmas cards to make gift tags for this year's presents.		Got an oily pizza box out of the recycling bin and put it in the compost bin.

Get others interested

You can make a poster or leaflets to show others how to recycle paper. Most people want to recycle their waste paper but are not sure how.

A bold heading will catch people's attention.

List the types of paper products that can be recycled.

PAPER RECYCLING

WHAT CAN BE RECYCLED?

List the types of paper products that cannot be recycled.

YES
- ✓ photocopy and office paper
- ✓ newspapers
- ✓ envelopes
- ✓ junk mail
- ✓ magazines
- ✓ telephone directories

NO
- ✗ books
- ✗ tissues
- ✗ thermal fax paper
- ✗ fluorescent paper
- ✗ pizza and food boxes
- ✗ soiled paper
- ✗ plastic- or wax-coated cardboard

You do not have to remove staples or plastic windows from envelopes. These are all removed during reprocessing.

You can help by sorting your papers at home. Do not put them in plastic bags.

HOW TO RECYCLE:

1 Keep papers dry.

2 Tie together large amounts of newspapers and magazines with twine.

3 Most non-recyclable paper can be composted at home.

Except for plastic-coated paper, cardboard, magazines, and white office paper because it contains chlorine.

Once paper has been wet it is harder to remove the ink.

 Thank you for recycling.

Add interest to your leaflets with pictures or computer clip art images.

Decomposition timeline

This timeline shows how long it takes for products and materials to break down and return to the soil when left exposed to air and sunlight.

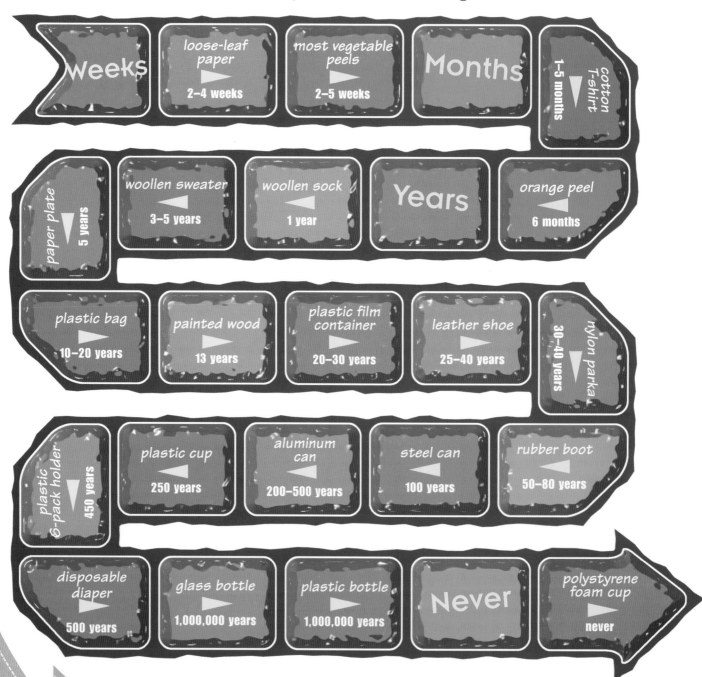

Weeks

loose-leaf paper
2–4 weeks

most vegetable peels
2–5 weeks

Months

cotton T-shirt
1–5 months

paper plate
5 years

woollen sweater
3–5 years

woollen sock
1 year

Years

orange peel
6 months

plastic bag
10–20 years

painted wood
13 years

plastic film container
20–30 years

leather shoe
25–40 years

nylon parka
30–40 years

plastic 6-pack holder
450 years

plastic cup
250 years

aluminum can
200–500 years

steel can
100 years

rubber boot
50–80 years

disposable diaper
500 years

glass bottle
1,000,000 years

plastic bottle
1,000,000 years

Never

polystyrene foam cup
never

Glossary

carbon a basic element of matter and the main element that living things are made of

carbon dioxide a gas breathed out by people and animals and taken in by trees, and also released by decomposing paper

chlorine a chemical used to bleach paper

compost decomposed plant and food waste, which is used to fertilize soil

contaminated ruined by harmful material; recycled paper can be contaminated by food, oil, or glue

decomposes breaks down into simple substances through the activity of tiny living organisms called bacteria

developed countries countries where most people have good living conditions and use a lot of manufactured products

emissions gases or small particles released into the atmosphere, such as methane gas released into the air by paper in landfills

fossil fuels fuels, such as petroleum, coal, and natural gas, which formed from the remains of ancient plants and animals

global warming warming of the Earth's atmosphere due to the build-up of heat-holding gases

grades different types of paper, such as white office paper or newsprint

habitats areas where particular plants and animals live and breed

humus decomposed material made from naturally occurring organic waste

incinerated burned in a closed container called an incinerator

insulation material that prevents heat from moving from one area to another

landfills large holes in the ground in which waste materials are buried

methane a gas released by decomposing paper in landfills

molecules very small pieces of a substance

natural resources materials taken from the Earth and used to make products, such as trees used to make paper

newsprint low-grade paper on which newspapers are printed

non-renewable cannot be made or grown again

organic made from or found in living things

paperboard stiff paper used in food packaging, such as cereal boxes

pollution dirty or harmful waste material that damages air, water, or land

pulp a soggy mix of water and small, solid particles of a substance, such as paper

pure streams lots of paper products made of exactly the same grade

raw materials materials that have not been processed or treated before, such as wood from trees

renewable can be made or grown again

reprocessed used paper again to make new paper products

Index